THE AMAZING
SPIDER-MAN

THE AMAZING SPIDER-MAN™

THE TANGLED WEBS OF SPIDER-MAN

TEN STORIES FROM THE FILM

ADAPTED BY NACHIE CASTRO, TOMAS PALACIOS, AND MICHAEL SIGLAIN
BASED ON THE SCREENPLAY BY JAMES VANDERBILT

MARVEL
NEW YORK

Printed in the United States of America

First Edition

1 3 5 7 9 10 8 6 4 2

V 475-2873-0-12092

ISBN 978-1-4231-5399-3

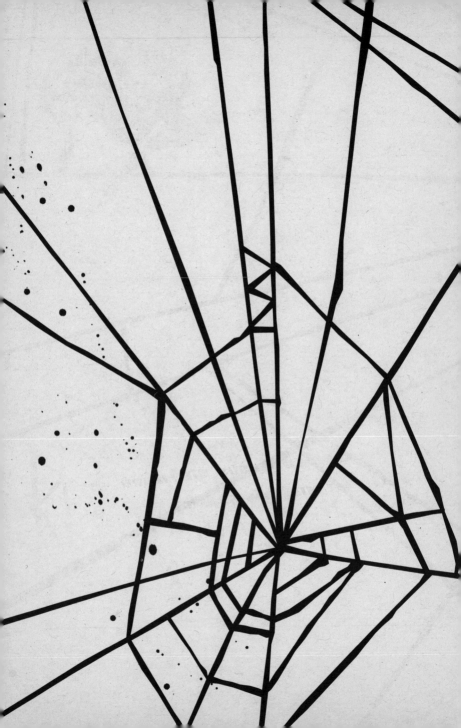

TABLE OF CONTENTS

STORY 1: **DOWN CAME THE RAIN** ... 1

STORY 2: **SCHOOL OF HARD KNOCKS** ... 13

STORY 3: **ALONG CAME A SPIDER** ... 23

STORY 4: **DISCOVERING NEW POWERS** ... 35

STORY 5: **WELL, THAT'S STRANGE** ... 45

STORY 6: **A CARTON OF EGGS** ... 55

STORY 7: **PLEASE PASS THE PEAS** ... 67

STORY 8: **THE BIGGEST TEST YET** ... 81

STORY 9: **SPIDER-MAN VERSUS THE LIZARD** ... 93

STORY 10: **BATTLE AT MIDTOWN SCIENCE HIGH** ... 105

THE AMAZING SPIDER-MAN™

THE **TANGLED WEBS** OF **SPIDER-MAN**

TEN STORIES FROM THE FILM

DOWN CAME THE RAIN

PETER PARKER RAN through the house as fast as he could, almost as if his life depended on it. The sound of his bare feet slapping against the hardwood floor echoed throughout the hallway. Turning a corner, he found himself in his parents' bedroom, staring at a picture of a man wearing glasses. The same glasses which sat, neatly folded, in front of the picture. But there was no time to stare at photos of sunny days or think about the spectacles that lay before him. Peter stepped toward the closet, but stopped in his tracks when a gust of wind from a half-open window blew rainwater into the house and shattered the glass windowpane.

In all his time playing hide-and-seek with his father, creeping around the house and concealing himself in unseen nooks and crannies within their home, Peter never felt scared. But the howling of the wind, the beating of the rain against the house, and the shattering of the glass had made him afraid. Now he didn't want to find his father to just win the game. He wanted to find his father to make sure everything was all right.

Peter ran even faster and soon appeared in his father's study, a room that was usually off-limits to the young boy. Broken glass littered the floor beneath the window, and two of his father's desk drawers appeared to have been overturned and emptied. Peter looked around at the large wooden desk and spotted something else odd: a large black spider—one unlike any he had ever seen before—suspended inside a bell jar on his dad's desk. The spider was long dead, but it still sent a shiver down Peter's spine.

Peter's fear grew as the sound of heavy footsteps filled his ears. As if from nowhere, Peter's father appeared in the doorway. He quickly surveyed the room, then roughly grabbed Peter by the elbow and pulled him into the hallway.

"Stay here," his father commanded. So he did.

Richard Parker worked quickly. He reached beneath the last desk drawer and pulled out a folder marked "OO." He tucked it under his arm just as his wife, Mary, arrived. They exchanged a knowing look, then turned their attention to Peter.

The next thing Peter knew, he was in the backseat of their car, which was racing down the road. The three of them had left so quickly that Peter's feet were still bare, a fact that had gone unnoticed by his mother, who was driving the car, and by his father, who was busy sorting the contents of his briefcase.

From the dark leather case, Peter's father produced a multicolored cube—a Rubik's Cube—and tossed it to his son in the backseat. Peter had never seen anything like it. He instantly began turning each side, mixing up the cube's colors.

The game occupied Peter's mind for the rest of the drive. Before he knew it, he was standing with his parents inside the home of his uncle and aunt in Forest

Hills, Queens. As the adults spoke in hushed tones, Peter's dad leaned down to talk to his son.

"You'll find it easy," Peter's dad said, referring to the Rubik's Cube. He then added, "You'll be staying with Aunt May and Uncle Ben for a little while."

"Where are you going?" Peter asked, confused.

"There is something your mom and I need to do. I need you to be a good boy."

Then Peter's parents started to say good-bye. "He'll only drink chocolate milk. And he doesn't like crust on his sandwiches and—" Mary said to May, her voice trailing off. Richard pulled at her. It was time to go.

Richard kneeled before his son one last time. "I was in the coatroom," Peter's dad began.

"I don't like that room," Peter said, unsure what was happening.

"That's why I hid there," Peter's dad said. "That's the secret to the game. Remember that. Be good, Peter."

Then Peter's dad handed his leather briefcase to his brother, Ben, hugged Peter tightly, and walked out into the rainy night.

"It's all right. Everything's going to be all right,"

Aunt May said reassuringly to Peter, who stared out into the stormy night and watched as his parents' car pulled away.

Peter's reflection in the rain-spattered window made it look as if he was crying, but he wasn't. He was being strong, even though he didn't want to be. Young Peter Parker was sad and confused, and he already missed his parents.

Twelve years later, all those memories came flooding back as Peter stood in the basement of Uncle Ben and Aunt May's house holding an object that, unbeknownst to Peter at the time, would hold the key to his future.

The refrigerator in the basement had broken, causing a bad leak. When Peter and Uncle Ben went to investigate, they attempted to salvage as many boxes from the flood as they could. Inside one of the boxes was a rectangular object that was caked with dust. When Peter ran his fingers over it, he felt an embossment which revealed the letters RP. Peter knew exactly what this was—his father's leather briefcase. The same briefcase that Richard Parker had given to Uncle Ben on that rainy night twelve years ago . . . the last time Peter saw his parents.

Peter was lost in thought when a calm but gruff voice brought him back to the present. "I was with your father when he bought that." It was Uncle Ben, and it was time to talk about Peter's parents.

Upstairs in the kitchen, Aunt May dried the dishes while Peter and Uncle Ben sifted through the contents of the briefcase. It contained a deck of playing cards, two pens, a picture of Peter's mother, and the same eyeglasses that Peter remembered seeing in his parents' room so many years ago.

"He was nineteen years old. Saw it in a store window, a leather shop on Ninth Avenue. Always wanted it. Never had enough money for it," Uncle Ben began. "But when he did have just enough, he went into that store and, quick as a wink, bought the thing. And you know who sold it to him? Your mother, Mary. A shopgirl with a summer job saving for college. I was there. I witnessed it. Love at first sight," Uncle Ben said with a melancholy smile as he thought about days gone by.

"He gave this to you the night he left," the now

teenaged Peter said to his uncle, trying to understand more about his parents and just why they left.

"He told me to keep it safe," Uncle Ben replied.

"Why?" Peter questioned. "There's nothing in here."

And that's when Aunt May interrupted. "Your father was a secretive man, Peter," she said, joining the conversation. But Peter was already eyeing the yellow edge of a news clipping that was peeking out of a stitched side pouch. The clipping showed a picture of Peter's father with a one-armed man in front of Oscorp Plaza in Manhattan. The clipping's caption read: DR. RICHARD PARKER STANDING OUTSIDE OSCORP TOWER.

"Do you know who this man is?" Peter asked, referring to the one-armed man. Peter was so focused on the clipping that he didn't notice Ben and May exchange worried looks.

"Someone my brother worked with, I suppose," Ben said, hoping to sound convincing.

Aunt May finished drying her hands, then walked over to the briefcase and stared at the picture of Mary. "Take it away," Aunt May said. "It makes me sad."

Later, Peter sat alone in his bedroom, inspecting the briefcase. Surely it would tell him something more about his father, and in turn, something about himself. Peter noticed his father's glasses and got an idea. He took one contact out of his eye, and slipped on his dad's glasses. Everything was perfectly clear. Did he and his dad have the same astigmatism? Was their vision identical? While Peter was contemplating these questions, he noticed his father's old Oscorp ID badge.

Peter lifted the badge to his face and studied it, particularly the picture of his father on the front. Richard Parker was wearing the same glasses that Peter now wore. The resemblance was uncanny. Peter Parker looked just like his father.

That's when Peter noticed the Rubik's Cube on his shelf—the other memento from the last night he had seen his parents. Peter walked over to it and gave the cube a few twists. Peter reflected on what happened when he was younger, and on the discovery that he had made earlier today. He knew that his own life, and the mystery of his parents' disappearance, was the ultimate puzzle to solve.

Peter went back to the briefcase and got to work, turning it over and over in his hands. Twisting it, he noticed something sliding inside the case. Peter dug deeper and found something just below the inside flap: a slim folder marked with a double helix and an infinity symbol. The mystery of Peter's father, and his briefcase, was deepening.

But before Peter could investigate the contents of the folder, a creak on the stairs alerted him to Uncle Ben's presence at his doorway. He looked up to see an awestruck Uncle Ben staring back at him.

"My God, but you look just like him," Uncle Ben said, referring to Peter wearing his father's eyeglasses. Then Uncle Ben took a deep breath and began a conversation that he had put off for quite some time. "I'm not an educated man, Peter. You know that. I stopped helping you with your homework when you were ten. What I'm saying is, I know it's been hard for you . . . not having him. He was a brilliant man. I know we don't talk about them much—"

"It's okay," Peter began, trying to reassure his uncle that everything was all right.

"No, it's not," Uncle Ben continued. "If I could change it—"

"I know who my parents are," Peter said definitely. Peter put his hand on Uncle Ben's shoulder and looked the man who raised him in the eye. Uncle Ben smiled, but he knew that he had to continue.

"Curt Connors," Uncle Ben began. "That's the man in the photograph. Your father worked with him. They were close. But after that night . . . he never called. Not once."

Peter studied Uncle Ben, weighing the information that was just imparted to him. In an instant, Uncle Ben was at the door, closing it and allowing Peter some time to himself.

Peter moved back to the briefcase and looked at it, the secret folder, and his father's glasses. He ended his gaze on a picture of Richard Parker. This was not the man who raised him, but his real father. What mysteries surrounded his leaving on that rain-soaked night? To Peter, this was the ultimate puzzle—one that he was determined to solve, now more so than ever.

Up until then, Peter Parker's life had been typical.

Ordinary. But now, deep down, Peter began to suspect that he was meant for something more. That his life would be anything but ordinary. Peter Parker suspected that some day he would be amazing.

And little did he know, he was right. . . .

STORY 2:

SCHOOL OF
HARD KNOCKS

THE BANNER ABOVE Peter's head read, MIDTOWN SCIENCE HIGH'S WALL OF CHAMPIONS, but it was the display case that interested Peter. Behind the glass were photographs of all of Midtown High's current champions: the basketball team, the football team, the volleyball team, and the chess club. And while all of the photographs were taken by Peter Parker, these were not what preoccupied Peter at the moment. Neither was the photograph of the debate team, which Peter was adding to the display. It was a particular person in the photograph that captured Peter's attention. Among the nearsighted girls and boys stood a golden-haired goddess. She was the captain of the debate team, and she was exquisite. She was Gwen Stacy, and she was the girl of Peter's dreams.

"That picture sucks, Parker," said a Neanderthal behind Peter. The Neanderthal's name was Flash Thompson, star athlete and Midtown High's resident bully.

"Actually, Flash, it's pretty flattering, given your strong simian features, which I addressed with a lens choice," Peter retorted. He knew that Flash wasn't talking about the picture of Gwen, but about the most recent picture of the football team.

"I'm talking about that!" Flash yelled as he pointed to the caption beneath the football team photo which read, EUGENE THOMPSON. "I haven't been Eugene since first grade!"

"Missy Kallenback does captions. She just follows policies," Peter said, trying to brush off the overzealous bully.

"I'm telling Coach. He'll fix it!" Flash said as he stormed off. With Flash gone, Peter walked to class, his mind lost in thought about Gwen. Later, at his locker, Peter heard a commotion coming from the quad, and immediately readied his camera.

. On his way to the noise, Peter spied Gwen sitting alone on the bleachers, her head in a book. Peter raised his camera and waited. Just as Gwen dropped her book, Peter snapped a picture. She was gorgeous! But before Peter could do or say anything, the commotion grew suddenly louder, and Peter set off to investigate.

Much to the delight of the hooting crowd, Flash Thompson was holding a fellow student by his ankles above a plate of spaghetti. "Eat your vegetables, Gordon!" Flash commanded.

"Actually, spaghetti is a complex carbohydrate," an upside-down Gordon corrected.

With that, the lunchroom broke out into a chant of, "Eat it! Eat it! Eat it!"

Peter sighed. This was just another typical day at Midtown High, and he had had enough. It was time to confront Flash once and for all, and it appeared that Peter was the one to do it. But when Peter appeared, Flash saw his arrival as yet another photo op for the school's number one photojournalist. "Hey, Parker, take a picture of this!" Flash said with a smile.

But Peter was not amused. "Put him down, Flash. Don't eat it, Gordon," Peter said defiantly.

Gordon didn't want a fight, he just wanted to be put down. "It's okay, Peter," he said. "Besides, except for pita pizza, this is the cafeteria's best dish."

That's when Flash interrupted, yelling to Peter to take the picture. Peter slowly raised his camera and framed the picture, but just before he snapped the shot, he turned and addressed the howling crowd. "I just want to make sure we're all okay with this. That we all want to celebrate Gordon's face being smothered in his own marinara. It seems a bit cruel to me. . . ."

The crowd grew quiet as Peter continued to fight for his cause. "It's Gordon. We love Gordon. I think he deserves better than being force-fed meatballs while being dangled upside down. Flash, this moment could really mess up my boy's future. Frankly, I think he could be president someday. . . ."

"No, I'm going to be a C.P.A., like my father," Gordon whispered to Peter, but Peter forged on, assured that he had the crowd behind him and that, for once, the underdogs would come out on top.

"Let's ask ourselves, do we chant mindlessly—egging on the ritual humiliations of the captain of our chess team? Or do we say, no, Gordon will not eat meatballs. Not here. Not today. Not ever."

There was a long awkward pause as Peter, Flash, and Gordon looked around the cafeteria. The silence was suddenly broken by a rousing chant of, "Eat it! Eat it! Eat it!" And with that, Peter knew that he had failed.

"You're alone, Parker," Flash said with a smirk.

"Put him down, Flash," Peter countered.

"Take. The. Picture." Flash said between gritted teeth.

"Put. Him. Down," Peter said, sure that he had everyone's attention before adding, "Eugene."

With a *plop*, Flash dropped Gordon into his plate of spaghetti and meatballs. And before he could react, before he even realized that he had pushed Flash just a little too far, Peter was on the floor, reeling from a powerful right cross to the jaw. Flash had hit Peter hard, and before Peter could truly comprehend what was happening, Flash was hitting him again.

The crowd cheered with delight as the fight

continued, though it was by no means a fair fight. Flash hit Peter again and again, repeatedly knocking him to the ground. Peter didn't know if Flash grew bored or tired, but the captain of the football team finally told Peter to stay down.

Giving in, Peter fell back to the ground as a triumphant Flash turned to face his adoring crowd. Instead, he came face-to-face with Gwen, who clearly wasn't happy with what was going on. As they and the rest of the crowd dispersed, Gordon made his way over to Peter.

Angry and humiliated, Gordon turned to Peter in tears. "Why'd you have to get involved? I would've just eaten it." Gordon left, and Peter was alone. He had failed. The underdogs had again lost, and now even Gordon was mad at Peter.

Peter was disappointed in himself. His whole head hurt, and to make matters worse, his camera had been broken in the fight. When the bell rang, Peter picked himself up and slowly made his way to class.

Peter walked into chemistry, happy to be in a class he liked and happier still to have found an empty seat directly behind Gwen Stacy. All thoughts of the fight, the pain, and his humiliation and disappointment were gone as he stared at the back of Gwen's head. The light bounced off of her perfect hair, onto her perfect neck, and onto her perfect face. Her face! Gwen Stacy was suddenly staring at Peter Parker!

"I thought it was great what you did," she began. "Stupid, but great. You should probably go to the school nurse. You may have a concussion." Peter was transfixed and sat in abject silence. Gwen Stacy was worried about him!

"What's your name?" she asked.

This stunned Peter and jolted him back to reality. "We've been going to school together for ten years," he said in disbelief.

"I know your name," she said flatly. "I want to see if *you* know your name."

"Peter. Parker," he said with a stammer.

"Correct," she said with a smile. "But I'd still go to the nurse." And with that, the perfect Gwen Stacy turned around in her seat to face the teacher. Peter sat in a state of euphoria.

"Gwen Stacy knows my name," he said softly to himself.

"I can hear you," Gwen replied.

Peter's bad day had turned into an excellent one. He might not have stopped the school bully or saved a student from being dropped into a plate of pasta, and his head might still be throbbing from taking a beating from Flash, and his camera might still be broken—but the girl of his dreams spoke to him, knew his name, and even complemented him. Peter Parker was so happy that he thought he could walk on walls, just like in that old movie musical. And if Gwen ever decided to go out with him then maybe, just maybe, one day, he would!

ALONG CAME A SPIDER

PETER PARKER STOOD inside the massive Oscorp Tower lobby and wondered how he was going to get by their security and get in to see Dr. Curtis Connors. Peter had spent the previous night scouring the Internet for information about Dr. Connors. He learned that his father's former colleague had won numerous awards for his scientific accomplishments, and had even written a best-selling book, *The Splice of Life*, about genetics and DNA. Peter also learned that Dr. Connors worked at Oscorp, which lead Peter to the impressive granite, steel, and glass lobby where he now stood. All the building's employees were using their security cards to pass into an elevator bay. Peter eyed the security guards in the corner, took a deep breath, and made his way toward the reception desk. It was now or never!

An attractive receptionist with deep blue eyes instantly sized him up. "You'll find yourself to the left," she said. This confused Peter. He looked to his left and noticed a table with numerous name tags arranged in a grid. "You *are* here for the internship?" the girl questioned.

Peter blinked twice and decided to play along. "Yes. Of course. Absolutely."

Then the receptionist began her routine: "Display badge at all times. Failure to do so will result in removal from the tour." Peter said nothing. This time she blinked twice. "Are you having trouble finding yourself?" she asked.

Peter grabbed the closest badge he could find, and the receptionist kept talking. "Please proceed to the east elevator, Mr. Guevara."

"Gracias . . . ?" Peter meekly replied as he glanced down at the name on his badge. It read: RODRIGO GUEVARA. He frowned to himself and quickly made his way over to the other interns. Just as Peter joined them, they all turned to look in his direction. But they weren't looking at him. They were looking past him, to the silhouette of a girl walking toward them holding a clipboard. The interns' glasses instantly fogged up. The chorus line of nerds parted to reveal the breathtaking beauty, and Peter could not believe his eyes. It was Gwen Stacy! Not wanting to be noticed, Peter put his head down and made his way to the back of the group.

"Welcome to Oscorp," Gwen said as she introduced herself to everyone. "I'm the head intern for Dr. Connors. I'll be with you for the duration of your visit. Where you go, I go. Remember that and we'll be fine."

But none of the interns moved a muscle. They were in awe of the gorgeous girl before them. "This is where we get in the elevator," Gwen whispered, calling them to action. Soon, they were on the forty-second floor, visiting the animal-dynamics lab. They stepped into Section A, and that's when Peter saw him.

"Welcome. My name is Dr. Curtis Connors. And yes, for those of you wondering, I am a southpaw." And with that, Peter turned his attention to Dr. Connors's right arm . . . or where his right arm would have been, had the good doctor not lost it years earlier. "I am not a cripple," Dr. Connors began. "I am a scientist and the world's foremost authority on herpetology—that's reptiles for those of you who don't know—but like the Parkinson's patient who watches in horror as her body slowly betrays her or the man with macular degeneration whose sight grows dimmer each day, I long to fix myself. And I'm here to tell you this will be achieved in my lifetime. Anyone care to venture a guess just how?"

A freckle-faced kid decided to hazard a guess, but was ultimately wrong. Dr. Connors good naturedly started to question Gwen about the intelligence of the group when an unseen intern spoke up. It was Peter Parker.

"Cross-species genetics," Peter said, and with that, both Dr. Connors and Gwen turned to see Peter step forward. "A person gets Parkinson's when the brain cells that produce dopamine start to disappear," he continued. "But the zebra fish can regenerate cells on command. If you could somehow give this ability to the woman you mentioned, she could cure herself."

"What about the man losing his sight?" Dr. Connors asked.

"It might not matter," Peter said confidently.

"I suspect he would disagree," Dr. Connors countered.

"Not if you could replace his visual abilities with something superior," Peter said. "A bat's sonar system is so sophisticated it doesn't need to see a tree to avoid it."

Dr. Connors studied Peter before finally asking him his name. But before he could answer, someone beat him to it . . . someone who already knew his name.

"He's from Midtown Science. Number two in his class," Gwen said as she eyed Peter. Dr. Connors moved in to speak with them, but was suddenly called away by an urgent telephone call. This left Peter face-to-face with Gwen, who wasn't happy to see him.

"Rodrigo . . . *hola,*" she said with ice in her voice. "What are you doing here?"

"What are *you* doing here?" Peter quickly replied.

"I work here," Gwen said matter-of-factly.

"I was going to say I work here, too, but I guess that's taken?"

"So . . . ?" Gwen said, not letting him off the hook for his lie.

"I'm an intern?" Peter joked.

"Strike two," Gwen replied. "Why are you follow-ing me?"

"How do I know *you're* not following *me*?" Peter said. He was having fun with this!

"Because this is where I work!" Gwen said with frustration.

"Maybe it's just a clever ruse. How long have you known Connors?" he asked.

"*Doctor* Connors," Gwen corrected him. "I've been here six months. Nice try with the zebra fish, by the way, but it'll take a whole lot more than cribbing choice tidbits from his book to impress him, you know."

"The bat wasn't in the book," Peter said, defending himself to the blond beauty before him.

Gwen turned and walked away, then turned back to look at Peter once more. He gave her a faint smile, and she looked him over again before addressing the rest of the interns. It was time for the remainder of the tour, but Peter had other plans and ducked away as soon as everyone's backs were turned.

Peter strode down a long, dimly lit hallway that

ended at a glass door. The plate next to the door was engraved with a double helix, just like the one he had seen in his father's notes. Peter pulled out his father's old Oscorp ID and slid it through the keypad. Access denied. He would need to find another way in. Like clockwork, the answer revealed itself in the form of two lab technicians. Peter quickly hid around the corner and watched as they entered a thirteen-digit code into the keypad.

Peter, having seen and remembered the code, immediately followed. As the doors to the lab whooshed open, Peter found himself inside what he would soon learn was an elaborate spider nursery. He was instantly awestruck. A low hum filled his ears as he entered, and the room appeared to float and shimmer. But upon closer examination, Peter learned the reason why the room looked the way it did: the walls were constructed from spiderwebs, which were so delicate that even Peter's breath caused them to tremble.

Suddenly, a loud CLICK-CLACK broke through the hum, startling Peter out of his stupor. Peter whirled around to see a sleek contraption with the crablike movements of a metal spider zip-lining into view and working its way across pegs that were studded into the wall. The machine was gathering all of the web-lines into one single filament.

The filaments were then stretched back and forth over Peter's head, as if the ceiling itself was a giant loom. The web-lines were now as strong as tightropes, and just when all of the strands were completed, the metal spider contraption scurried up the wall and into the ceiling as the filaments disappeared into a side panel. Then all was quiet. Still.

Without warning, small white pellets started to gush from the side panel as if they were a wave of shiny metal pearls. Peter examined one, and pocketed it for further inspection. Then Peter heard the two lab techs again and panicked. He surely wasn't meant to be in here. Peter whirled around to head for the door—and accidentally disturbed a pair of silken web-lines . . . which caused two dozen strange spiders to fall from the ceiling onto his head and shoulders.

Peter freaked out, but he couldn't scream, otherwise the lab techs would hear him, so he froze.

Slowly, the eerie arachnids crawled over his head, neck, and shoulders, their eight legs softly moving over his goose-bumped skin. Peter couldn't take it any longer!

Peter flailed his arms wildly and jumped up and down, doing a mad, but silent, dance to get the spiders off him. But he had to be careful. He couldn't make any noise. He also didn't want to hurt any of the spiders, since they were clearly lab specimens. Peter continued to jump about until all the spiders were off him and on the floor. They scattered in all directions. Just as Peter was about to catch his breath, he heard the lab techs again. That was it! Peter had had enough and knew that he had to get out of the lab!

But unbeknownst to Peter, one small spider had clung to him, and slowly made its way down from his head to his neck. This spider looked just like that strange specimen Peter's father kept in the bell jar on his desk. The spider lied in wait on Peter's collar, ready to strike.

Peter dashed out of the lab and walked as fast as he could down the hallway. He saw the two lab techs coming his way, so he put his head down and walked even faster. "They get younger every year," one tech said to the other as Peter quickly passed by.

The elevator door opened and Peter threw himself inside, finally taking a moment to catch his breath. But it would only be for a moment, for when the elevator doors opened, Gwen Stacy was waiting for him. "Give it to me," she demanded. Peter was once again confused.

Then he remembered the name tag, and slowly passed "Rodrigo Guevara" back to Gwen Stacy. Gwen turned and marched off to the other interns, and as she did, the spider on Peter's collar slowly made its way across his neck. Just as Gwen turned to give him one last look, the spider revealed its glistening white fangs and dug them deep into the back of Peter's neck!

"Ow!" Peter yelled at the sudden pain. At the sound of his cry, Gwen gave him one last suspicious look, then turned away and directed her attention back to the other interns. Her real interns.

Peter moved his hand across the back of his neck and felt a welt. Something had pinched him. Or maybe even bitten him. He didn't know what, and right now, he didn't care. He was in the lobby of Oscorp Tower, and he just wanted to leave.

Peter had gone to Oscorp Tower to learn more about Dr. Connors—the man who worked with his father—in an attempt to learn more about his father. Instead, Peter came away with even more questions. Peter's mind was reeling. He admired Dr. Connors and thought that he might have even impressed him. He wondered what Dr. Connors would say if he knew just who Peter was, that he was the son of Richard Parker. But Peter hadn't expected to run into Gwen Stacy, the girl of his dreams. And he certainly hadn't expected to find himself in some sort of high-tech spider nursery.

But Peter couldn't think about any of that now. He felt suddenly strange, as if his whole body was tingling. A wave of tiredness washed over him as the welt on his neck throbbed. Peter just wanted to go home and sleep. He would have to figure out the mystery of who he was, and who his parents were, another day. He was sure that after a little rest, everything would become clear.

And yet Peter Parker was wrong. His average life was about to get very complicated . . . and very amazing.

DISCOVERING NEW POWERS

WHAT'S THE CHANCE that anyone in New York has had a more eventful day than this one? thought Peter Parker. In the past couple of hours, he had gone to Oscorp and met one of the world's most brilliant scientists—who just happened to have worked with Peter's father. *And* he had talked to Gwen Stacy, the girl he'd had a crush on for years. Even better, he really talked to her, not just an "excuse me" as he went from class to class. Granted, he had been bitten by a spider in Oscorp, which also didn't happen every day, but he wasn't about to let a tiny spider ruin his day.

He slumped into an empty subway seat on his train home, dropping his backpack and skateboard between his legs. The subway car had barely begun moving, and the conductor's voice had just finished saying, "Queens-bound F. The next stop is . . ." before Peter fell asleep. And he fell asleep *hard*. What Peter didn't yet realize was the spider that had bit him was no ordinary spider. It was part of a secret Oscorp experiment altering the DNA of animals. Somehow, the spider's altered DNA was also tweaking Peter's DNA.

Peter, of course, had no way of knowing any of this. All he knew was that he was sweating, his hands were kinda clammy, and he really needed a nap. He slept through his subway stop in Queens, and he slept through the train getting to the end of the line and heading back the way it came. He slept as the train headed back, past his stop in Queens again and into Manhattan—and past the stop next to the Oscorp building in Midtown. He even kept sleeping as the train rattled into Brooklyn, rolling toward the edge of the city as the sun set.

Normally, a bunch of loud and rowdy people getting close to Peter would have gotten his attention. But not this time. "I ruled today!" said the first of guys who got onto the train. They had a football and a bunch of bottles with them, and it looked like they'd been enjoying both for a while. "Did I rule, Sheila?" he asked one of the girls who were hanging out with him and his friends.

"That's you, Troy. You're the king," Sheila said while rolling her eyes. The train shook as it rolled along, and Troy bumped into Peter's backpack, but Peter didn't stir at all. "Whoa, check this guy out," said Troy, leaning over Peter. He turned to his friends and pointed at Peter. "He's out cold! Watch this. . . ."

Troy took one of the bottles and gently balanced it on Peter's head. Troy's buddies laughed and clapped; Peter was still dead asleep. One of the drops of condensation rolled down the bottle, traveled all the way down the barrel of the bottle, and went *plip*, right against Peter's forehead. The instant the cold water touched him, Peter's eyes shot open! Like someone waking from a nightmare, he shot to his feet, but he didn't stop there. Peter kept on moving, and with lightning speed, he crawled *up* the side of the subway car's wall, all the way to the ceiling. As he crouched there, on the ceiling, upside down, he looked at Troy, Sheila, and the rest of their group staring at him with their mouths wide open. His heart was racing at what felt like a million beats a minute and everything around him looked like it was moving in slow motion.

He barely had time to think, *What is going on?* before two things tumbled to the ground: the bottle that had been resting on his head, and Peter himself. Liquid flew from the bottle, hitting Sheila, just as Peter got to his feet. "You moron!" she yelled at Troy, mad at him for putting the bottle on poor Peter's head to begin with.

Troy was confused at both what he had just seen, and also at Sheila's reaction. "What'd I do?"

Meanwhile, Peter was finally starting to get his bearings. "I—I'm sorry," he stammered. "I didn't mean to . . ." he reached out to Sheila to apologize, but when his fingers brushed her shoulder, the fabric of her shirt stuck to his hands. "Gah!" he yelled, panicking, and he jerked his hand away.

Later that night, safely back at home and thinking back to the events on the subway, Peter realized this was the exact moment where things *really* got out of control.

When Peter jerked his hand away from Sheila's

shoulder, her shirt stayed with Peter's hand, instead of staying on Sheila's body. For a moment, there was dead silence; it seemed to Peter as if even the subway had stopped making any noise. There was just him, holding a strange woman's shirt. Sheila stood shocked in a tank top, and Troy and the other guys surrounded Peter on the train. Then Sheila screamed, and Troy, his face turning red, started yelling at Peter. "Are you kidding?!? Are you freaking kidding?!?" Peter was trying to apologize to everyone at the same time as he was staring at his hand, trying to shake off Sheila's shirt, and so Peter barely noticed that Troy's giant fist was headed toward Peter's head.

Without even thinking about it, Peter's arm shot up and blocked Troy's punch. Man, I really wish I could let go of this woman's shirt, was the only thing that went through Peter's mind. And then Troy's two guy friends got involved.

As the train rolled through the tunnels beneath New York, Peter was in the middle of the biggest and weirdest fight he had ever seen. Troy tried to catch Peter in a bear hug, but Peter slithered out of the way.

Troy's friend tried to punch Peter in the back of his head, but Peter felt a buzzing at the base of his neck and instinctively moved in the nick of time. Every time one of the guys tried to jab, kick, scratch, poke, uppercut, head-butt, grab, or even touch Peter, he would effortlessly move out of the way. Troy grabbed Peter's skateboard from the floor and swung it as hard as he could, aiming right at Peter's head.

Peter quickly and easily brought his arm up to block the blow. The arm that didn't have Sheila's shirt in it, that is. He was moving so fluidly that he had time to think: I really hope that guy doesn't try to steal my board; I don't think I can afford another one. And, Oh, hey, there's a good chance this is really going to hurt . . . all before the skateboard even hit his arm. The good news was it definitely didn't hurt. Peter barely felt the board hitting him. The bad news was, Troy was pretty strong after all. Strong enough so, combined with Peter's suddenly supertough forearm, the skateboard broke in half from the impact with a loud CRACK!

Once again, everyone in the subway car was stunned into silence. Peter stood still, breathing heavily, waiting for one of the guys to try and hit him again—but they didn't move. All of a sudden, the subway's speakers broke the silence: "Next stop, Coney Island," echoed from the train, as it lurched to a stop and the doors opened. Just as Peter's heartbeat started to slow down, Sheila's shirt finally fell out of his hand. In one motion, Peter caught the shirt again before it hit the floor, tossed it at Sheila, grabbed his backpack, and sprinted out the doors into the evening, leaving behind a group of very surprised people standing around an empty bottle and a broken skateboard.

Peter sprinted from the train's platform and down the stairs, heading to the street. His mind was buzzing with unanswerable questions. What just happened? How did that guy break my skateboard? Why were they moving so slowly? Wait, was I moving really fast? Why did that woman's shirt stick to my hand? Wait, was her shirt sticking to my hand, or was my hand sticking to her shirt? When did it get dark out? Am I in Coney Island? How did that happen? Wasn't I just getting on the train from Oscorp? I'm starving. Maybe I have time to get a hot dog. No! Aunt May and Uncle Ben are going to kill me for being so late. Should I get back on the train? There's no way I'm getting on another train for a while. I'm still running as fast as I can, shouldn't I be getting tired by now?

That last thought really made Peter wonder. He had been sprinting faster than he had ever been able to run before, and he'd been doing it for at least a mile. But he was barely even breathing heavily. He wasn't tired at all. Hungry? Yes. But not tired. Okay, let's think about this for a second, he thought. Forest Hills is northeast of here. I've lived in New York my whole life. I think I can find my way home. And with that, he took off into the night at full speed. Peter had no idea what was happening to him, but he knew he wanted to get home. He wanted to see his Aunt May and Uncle Ben, to let them know he was all right. Whatever answers he needed could wait until he was back home, safe and sound.

Was I on the ceiling?

STORY 5:

WELL, THAT'S STRANGE

BY THE TIME Peter stopped running, night had fallen. He was very tired and extremely hungry. After all, it had been a weird day for the teenager. He got bit by a strange spider while at Oscorp, climbed to the ceiling of a subway car and then proceeded to stick there, upside down, and had just ran all the way to Forest Hill, Queens—from Coney Island, Brooklyn!

He walked up to the front door of Uncle Ben and Aunt May's home. The wind howled, and Peter's stomach growled louder and louder with each step he took. He quietly opened the door and made his way in but stopped dead in his tracks. There, standing in their bathrobes, were his aunt and uncle. They had been waiting all night for him! Aunt May and Uncle Ben stared at Peter, who looked very disheveled. His hair was a mess, his clothes were filthy and full of sweat, and he looked like he hadn't slept in days.

After a few seconds, Peter broke the awkward silence. "Sorry I'm late. Ran all the way."

"From where?" a confused Uncle Ben asked.

"Coney Island."

Another awkward pause.

"We were worried sick, Peter," Aunt May interjected.

"I'm sorry," Peter replied. "I just—watch out!"

With the utmost clarity, Peter watched a fly buzz by Aunt May's nose, as if in slow motion. So slow, he could see the flutter of the wings go up and down. Then, with incredible speed, he snatched the fly right out of midair. A stunned Aunt May and Uncle Ben watched as Peter stood there, holding the tiny bug between the tips of his fingers.

"That's a *fly*, Peter," Aunt May said in awe.

"So it is," Peter stated, gently examining the fly. "So it is." Then he let the bug go and it quickly buzzed away. "I'm sorry. I know I'm late. . . . Irresponsible. Insensitive . . . I'm hungry—"

Suddenly, Peter made a beeline for the kitchen, kissing Aunt May on her cheek on his way. This caught her off-guard, as she was still thinking about how Peter just caught a fly with his fingertips! He opened the refrigerator and grabbed the first thing he saw: Aunt May's world-class meat loaf. Peter sat at the kitchen table and began shoveling the food into his mouth. His aunt and uncle could only watch. At this point, it didn't make sense to ask any more questions.

"Your meat loaf beats all other meat loaves!" Peter mumbled as pieces of food fell from his mouth.

But he wasn't done. Peter got up and dived back into the refrigerator, pulling out everything in sight.

"Chicken. Coleslaw. Apple pie. Ice cream. À la mooode!" He chuckled gleefully, a huge smile running across his face. He laid out the entire contents of the fridge across the table and began to ravage a piece of chicken. There was enough food on the table to feed all three of them—twice. Peter's aunt and uncle glanced at each other, confused and a bit concerned. They wanted to ask Peter what had happened, but he was too caught up in his eating.

Then, Peter stood up, grabbed some food off the table, and began to make his way up to his room, munching on a piece of apple pie the entire way. Aunt May and Uncle Ben stood in the doorway of the kitchen and watched Peter go up the stairs and close his bedroom door behind him. Silence. They gazed at each other in confusion. Then they peered back into the kitchen, observing the spread of food left on the table. What had gotten into their nephew?

"Drinking?" Aunt May said, still staring at the mess of food.

Uncle Ben shook his head. "I don't think so."

"A girl?"

"Don't know," Uncle Ben said calmly. "Coney Island is twenty-seven miles away."

"So far. So fast," Aunt May said.

"So hungry," Uncle Ben added.

Peter entered his room and turned on the light. He placed his hands on his bloated stomach and realized how much he had actually eaten. Granted, Peter was a teenager and a high school student, so maybe this was normal, right? Peter rolled his neck and stretched a bit before stepping in front of his mirror. He studied his body for a minute before letting out a sigh. Same old Peter.

Peter began to turn away from the mirror when the light from the lamp illuminated something odd clinging to the back of his neck. He turned and saw a delicate piece of silk resting on his flesh, pulsing with his beating throat. Gently, Peter lifted the silk, surprised at its incredible strength. He followed the translucent thread over his shoulder and down into his shirt pocket. Peter looked in the mirror and paused. *What could it be?* Peter was pretty freaked out, but he had to know what it was. He reached in. He felt something tiny, too tiny to have noticed at any other time during the day. Then he pulled it out. It was a spider. The spider was tethered to the thin thread, but dead. And there was something oddly familiar about the small spider. It resembled the one he saw back in his father's office when he was a kid.

Peter studied the arachnid, its various colors illuminated in the light. He rotated the spider and took in its beauty. How could something so small be so amazing? Peter glanced back into the mirror and let out another sigh. It had been a crazy and hectic day, but he was too exhausted to try and make any sense of it now. He placed the spider down on his desk, got in his bed, and went to sleep.

The next morning, Peter awoke to the piercingly loud sound of his alarm clock. He hated that clock. It not only reminded him that he had to get up very early, but that he had to get up very early and go to school. Peter loved school, but still, he was a teenager and he'd rather be doing something else, such as skateboarding or taking pictures. He reached over and swung his arm to silence the clock. On any other day this would have worked. But today it worked too well. Peter whacked the clock and it shattered into a hundred pieces! He sat up and looked at his hand in confusion. Did that just happen?

Groggy and still exhausted from the events the

night before, Peter made his way to the bathroom. He picked up his toothbrush and toothpaste. As he squeezed the tube of blue mint paste onto his toothbrush, the entire contents of the tube shot out in one single blast and splattered across the mirror. I'm not that strong, he thought as he frowned at the empty tube. He grabbed some toothpaste off the mirror. As he began to brush his teeth, he turned the cold-water faucet on—but he accidentally twisted the faucet completely off, spraying water into the air like a geyser, soaking everything in the bathroom. Peter looked around frantically. What's going on here? He had to clean this up before Aunt May found out. He reached for the towel rack. Peter got the towel, but he also pulled the towel rack—and a bit of the bathroom wall—off as well. There he stood, in the semidestroyed bathroom, taking in all he had just done in a matter of seconds. Peter took a deep breath and ever-so-gently twisted the "off" valve under the sink, causing the spraying water to slowly descend and eventually stop. Peter exhaled. He did it. He looked in the mirror. Today is going to be an interesting day, he thought. He turned and left the bathroom, closing the door behind him . . . breaking off the doorknob in the process.

Uncle Ben had an easier time getting ready for his day. He got up, dressed for work, ate breakfast, and headed out the front door. But something caught his eye as he made his way down the stone path to the sidewalk. He could feel something behind him that wasn't right. When he turned, he saw what it was. There was Peter. Reading a book. On top of the roof.

"How in blazes did you get up there?" Uncle Ben asked oddly.

Peter was reading Dr. Connors's book, *Splice of Life*, while also looking over his father's notes that he found in the briefcase. He peered down to Uncle Ben. "Huh? Oh . . . I climbed."

Uncle Ben opened his mouth to reply, but after the events of last night, it probably was best to not ask. Instead, he nodded and headed off to work. As Uncle Ben disappeared from view, Peter quickly gazed through the last chapter of Connors's book—titled "The Final Question." He read the following:

$x/y =$? Until we solve this proportion; the

possibilities of controlling cross-species genetics will always remain out of reach.

Peter looked over his father's notes and concentrated on what had been circled. It read:

$$X/Y = \text{SPECIES LIFE SPAN}$$

Peter stared at those words. It meant something—but he was going to be late for class if he didn't leave now. Peter gathered his books, climbed down from the roof, and began his walk to school, his mind lost in thoughts about science—and his newfound strength. Yes, today was going to an interesting day indeed. . . .

When Peter Parker was a young boy, he liked to play hide-and-seek with his dad.

Ten years later, Peter is all grown up but still likes to hide, this time behind his camera from his high school crush, Gwen Stacy.

Flash Thompson, the star athlete and school bully, enjoys causing trouble for Peter.

One day, Peter discovers his father's old briefcase. Inside is a photo of Dr. Connors, a scientist that works at Oscorp.

Peter goes to Oscorp Tower to learn more about Dr. Connors but discovers Gwen Stacy is the head intern there!

At Oscorp, Peter finally meets Dr. Connors. Peter hopes to learn more about how Connors knew his dad.

Peter doesn't realize it yet, but the brilliant Dr. Connors will soon transform into the menacing *LIZARD*.

Peter struggles with being both an average teenager and the Amazing Spider-Man. But he remembers what Uncle Ben taught him: **WITH GREAT POWER COMES GREAT RESPONSIBILITY.**

After sneaking into an Oscorp lab, Peter is bitten by a strange spider—and develops even *STRANGER POWERS*.

After Peter created his costume, he invented *WEB-SHOOTERS* to help him swing through the city.

Hiding underground in the sewers of New York, Dr. Connors works in his secret lab on a dangerous experiment.

After Uncle Ben's murder, Peter searches for his killer—but he keeps this a secret from Aunt May.

With his new super powers and confidence, Peter finally gets the girl of his dreams—Gwen Stacy!

Ready for action, Peter hunts for the Lizard through the streets of New York City as *THE AMAZING SPIDER-MAN!*

A CARTON
OF EGGS

A SHADOW CREPT across the rooftops of New York City, silhouetted against the backdrop of the famous skyline. It was the shadow of a majestic new figure. A shadow that had a responsibility to fulfill. This shadow was Spider-Man!

And then his cell phone rang.

Total buzz kill, Peter thought.

"Hi, Aunt May," he said, picking up the call. "Yes, I promise to pick up eggs on my way home." Peter sighed. With Uncle Ben gone, Peter knew he had to help Aunt May any way he could. But picking up a carton of eggs was the least of his worries.

Peter put the cell phone away. It was hard trying to get used to this new suit he had made. It was skintight and did not leave a lot of room for normal accessories, such as a cell phone—or a carton of eggs for that matter. But, nonetheless, it would have to work, for now. Peter, in his new identity as the Amazing Spider-Man, had some unfinished business to handle with a thug on the street below.

A row of expensive cars lined the dark Lower Manhattan avenue. A man dressed in all black moved quietly to one of the luxurious automobiles. He peered around to see if anyone was watching. He smiled, thinking he was safe. The thief pulled out a digital decoder and fixed it over the vehicle's high-tech entry lock. As the decoder went to work, something flickered across the driver's side window. The thief quickly turned. He looked left. He looked right. Nothing. Suddenly, the thug heard a familiar "beep" and knew the car was now unlocked. Not so high-tech after all, he thought. He swung open the driver's side door, when suddenly a loud THUMP rang out nearby. Growing paranoid, the thief stepped away from the car and tried to find the origin of the unfamiliar sound. Again, he looked left, then right. But what he should have done was look *up*.

The thief returned to the vehicle and slid inside the driver's seat. Another smile. He had done it again and was about to get away in another stolen vehicle. Then he checked the rearview mirror and found Spider-Man sitting in the backseat.

"Who are you?" the thief said, surprised.

"The guy not stealing a car," Spider-Man said. "Okay, now you go. . . ."

"What are you? A cop?"

Really? Spidey thought. "That's right. I'm a cop wearing a skintight red-and-blue suit and a mask." Peter rolled his eyes behind his disguise. "With a mind like that, it's incredible how you haven't seized total control of the criminal underworld by now."

The thief stumbled out of the car and began to flee. But Spider-Man was one step ahead of him. The web-crawler quickly flipped the thief with his legs and the thug landed hard on the pavement. He recovered, then pulled out a blade.

"Bad idea," Spider-Man said as he moved in. Spidey raised his arms, flexed his wrists, and WHOOSH! Two web-cords fired out of his mechanical shooters and pinned the thug to a nearby brick wall. Even Spider-Man was taken aback by how awesome it was!

If the thief had been scared before, now he was terrified. "What is this?" he cried. "Help!"

"Be quiet!" Spider-Man hissed, scared that they'd be seen. He was still new to this Super Hero thing and wasn't sure how people would react to a guy wearing a spider suit.

The thief tried to scream once again, "HEEEELLLLLLL—" but Spider-Man cut him off by webbing his mouth shut. The thief's face began to turn a deep red. Spidey realized that maybe his webbing worked a little too well and walked over to him. He pulled up the thug's sleeve to see if there was a tattoo of a star—the tattoo that would help him find Uncle Ben's killer. But there was nothing.

"It's your lucky day," Spider-Man said to the thief, who was now pomegranate red. "Hold still." Spidey pulled his arm back as if ready to strike the thug who closed his eyes in fear. Then, with wicked fast reflexes, Spider-Man poked two nostril holes in the webbing for the thug to breathe from. "You're welcome."

Suddenly, a spotlight bleached the wall. Dozens of cops began coming out of nowhere, closing in on Spider-Man from all sides. One cop raised his weapon. "Don't move!" The officer squinted and realized what he was actually talking to. "Who are you?"

Spider-Man sighed. "Does nobody grasp the concept of the mask?"

"Drop your . . . weapon?" the confused cop said.

"I don't have a weapon. See, this is really more of a defense device," Spider-Man said as he raised his wrist to show the cop his webbing apparatus. But the officer just saw aggression and did what he was trained to do: he opened fire. With lightning speed, Spidey ticked left and watched the bullet whistle by. He aimed his web-shooter and tried to web the cop. But all he heard was CLICK. He was out of webbing! Spider-Man turned and ran.

Spidey raced down a dark elevated street and reloaded his web-shooter from his hip. He looked around for some place to shoot his web and swing out of danger, but there wasn't any. Spider-Man was grounded. Still running, he looked behind him and saw several cops in pursuit, their guns drawn.

"Stop! Or I'll shoot!" yelled one officer.

In one swift motion, Spider-Man raised his right hand and fired a web-cord onto the side railing of the elevated street. He leaped up and over with an aerial flip, twisted around in midair, and landed underneath the raised street bridge. Next, Spider-Man swung down to the street below. But he accidentally swung into oncoming traffic! Spider-Man tried to maneuver out of the way, but he was clipped by an oncoming bus. He rolled on his side and quickly recovered. On the upswing, he fired his web to a nearby building and made the new line shorter, pulling himself up and above the roofs of oncoming cars. With a sigh of relief and out of harm's way, Spider-Man swung through the valleys of New York, disappearing into the night. It seemed his new powers would take getting used to . . . and some practice.

Peter arrived at Aunt May's home. He quickly took off his Spider-Man suit and placed it in his backpack. Peter rattled open the back door a bit louder than he intended. There stood Aunt May at the stove, in her bathrobe, adjusting the flame under a tea kettle. The scene was very familiar to both Peter and Aunt May. The only thing missing this time was Uncle Ben.

Peter stood in the kitchen, not sure what to do. Head to his room? Hug Aunt May? Head back out to try and find Uncle Ben's killer? Instead, he simply said the name of the woman who had cared and been there for the past twelve years.

"Aunt May."

She didn't respond. Instead, Aunt May carried on making her tea, heading toward the cupboard to grab a tea bag.

"You don't need to wait up for me . . ." Peter said.

"Yes. I do," she said firmly. "Where have you been?"

"Around." He stared at the floor, too ashamed to look her in the eyes.

Aunt May looked him up and down, her eyes burning through his soul, searching for an answer of some sort. But she stopped, growing weary of this game. Instead she asked him if he completed the simple task she had given him earlier in the day. "Did you remember the eggs?"

Peter closed his eyes, kicking himself. How could he forget the one thing she asked for! "I'll go out now."

"No. You most certainly will not go out now," Aunt May said sternly. "Not at this time. Not now." She noticed something about his face that was not right. "Step into the light."

Peter slowly stepped forward, the light falling across his battered face. Several bruises. A gash under his eye. A busted lip.

Her old eyes grew sad. "Where is it you go, Peter? Who does this to you?"

"Go to sleep, Aunt May."

"I can't sleep!" she cried back. "Do you not understand that for thirty-eight years I have shared a bed with one man? Do you know what it's like after thirty-eight years to be alone?"

"No," he whispered, still unable to look her in the eyes.

Aunt May gazed across the empty kitchen then closed her eyes. For a just a moment, she remembered the happiness she shared with the man she would call her soul mate. Aunt May had fallen in love with Uncle Ben, married him, grew old with him, and stood by his every breath. They embodied what love is. But now, there was just pain. Loneliness. Silence. She shook her head at Peter, then stared at him, vaguely, as if looking right through him, lost in thought.

"He talked in his sleep, your uncle. I murdered him a thousand times over the years, lying awake waiting for him to grow quiet. Now I lie awake praying to hear his voice one more time."

Peter had no response. What could he say, really? There he stood just a few feet from Aunt May, unable to grasp the deafening silence between them. But that deafening silence was interrupted by the mournful wailing of the teakettle, as it reached its boiling point and cried out into the night. A cry of personal loss. A cry Peter knew all too well. The wailing rose higher and higher, but Aunt May just stared, doing nothing to silence the kettle. Having heard enough, Peter stepped forward to remove the pot from the heat, but Aunt May's eyes locked on Peter, cutting through the air like a knife. It was as if she wanted him to hear this cry.

Then, she removed the kettle from the flame, it's wailing dying down into the night. There was silence once more.

"Go to bed, Peter. Lay your head down. For a few hours you won't have to guard your secrets." She turned and started to head out of the kitchen. "But know this: the world is always listening. And everyone talks in their sleep . . ." Then Aunt May turned and walked away, leaving Peter alone in the quiet and desolate kitchen.

Peter wanted to run to Aunt May and hug her, tell her everything was going to be all right. He wanted to tell her that he was searching for Uncle Ben's killer. That he would not quit until justice was served. But Peter knew that even if justice was served, it would not bring Uncle Ben back . . . That was something not even Spider-Man could do. . . .

But Peter would eventually try and make it up to Aunt May. One day Aunt May came home after shopping at the local grocery store. She opened the refrigerator to put away some vegetables when she found that Peter had finally gotten her that carton of eggs he promised her . . . and he added an additional fifty-eight cartons, in case he forgot again. Aunt smiled and sighed. Perhaps Peter was learning after all . . .

PLEASE PASS THE PEAS

ACROSS TOWN, high above the streets of the Upper West Side of Manhattan, Gwen Stacy sat alone in her bedroom, thinking about a certain someone. A certain someone that made her smile. Suddenly, there was a light knock outside her window. Thinking it might be a bird pecking at the glass, she walked over to the window to shoo it away. Instead, she drew the curtain back and found that "someone" she had been thinking about sitting on the outside ledge of the high rise.

"Peter?" she said as she opened the window. "How did you get up here?"

"Fire escape. Your doorman is intimidating," he said nonchalantly.

Gwen looked down to the street far below then back at Peter. "It's twenty floors. . . ."

"Exactly. No big deal . . . Oh"—he pulled out a bouquet of flowers from his backpack—"these are for your mom . . ." But when Peter handed them to Gwen, several of the petals had fallen off and a few stems were broken.

Gwen grinned. "Lovely."

"Maybe not," Peter said, closing his backpack, a bit embarrassed.

She peered into the bag. "You have your suit in there too?"

Peter froze. "Suit?"

He wasn't sure how Gwen would react if he told her he had been bitten by an arachnid, developed superhuman powers, could climb up walls like a spider, and wore a one-piece leotard that made him look like an extra from Cirque du Soleil. But Gwen was referring to another suit. "It's dinner, Peter. I mean, you're not going to wear that?" she said, eyeing his jeans and wrinkled T-shirt.

Peter opened his mouth to say something, but there

was nothing to be said. What was he going to do? Tell her he'd be right back, then jump back out the window and swing home to grab a sports jacket? Gwen let him hang for a few seconds, and then a few more, until finally she smiled.

Peter breathed a sigh of relief. "Nice."

Suddenly there was a knock at her door, and now it was Gwen's turn to look nervous. The door opened and a tall man entered. He wore a crisp, clean outfit. His shirt was tucked in, his pants were pressed, and his shoes were unscuffed. The man's hair was perfectly combed down to the last strand. His face resembled that of someone who had seen a lot over the years and could point out a weasel, liar, or troublemaker just by looking at their clothes. This was Police Captain George Stacy—Gwen's father.

Captain Stacy observed Peter, as if trying to read his entire life. Then he broke the silence. "You must be Peter."

"Dad, this is Peter," Gwen said trying to ease the awkward tension.

Both men continued staring at one another.

From downstairs, Gwen's mother, Helen, called, "Dinner is almost ready. I hope you like branzino."

"Who doesn't?" Peter said, breaking the silence and heading out of the bedroom and down to the dining room.

At the Stacy family dinner, Peter sat between Gwen and her youngest brother, Simon, who was ten years old. Phillip, fifteen, and Howard, twelve, sat directly across from them. Captain Stacy and his wife, Helen, sat at each end of the rather large dinner table. It was the perfect family gathering—something you would see in a Lifetime film. This was new to Peter, who was used to sitting with Aunt May and Uncle Ben in their small Queens kitchen, joking about the day's events while eating Aunt May's world-class meat loaf. But not today. No, today Peter would be introduced to the branzino: a European silver-skinned fish usually lightly seasoned and then brazed, served with the head still attached. Peter peered at his plate warily.

Captain Stacy folded his hands and looked over at Phillip. "You can say grace."

"I haven't got one in me, Dad," Phillip stated.

Captain Stacy looked over at a puzzled Peter who was still looking down at his branzino. "Perhaps you'd like to."

Peter broke his death stare with the branzino and looked up in a state of panic. "Excuse me?"

The captain repeated himself, with a little more annunciation this time. "Perhaps you'd like to say grace?"

"Of course he doesn't want to say grace, George," Helen said, saving Peter and looking over at her son. "Howard . . . you do it."

As Howard lowered his head and closed his eyes, Peter followed along with the rest of the family, who started folding their hands and closing their eyes.

For a few seconds there was complete silence, until little Howard started his prayer. "It's the potholes. I've been doing a report on potholes. In the city. There are eighty-nine potholes between this apartment building and school. By counting them I lose fifteen minutes getting to school . . . which is why I have detention next week—amen."

Silence. Peter opened one eye and saw everyone looking toward the captain.

Captain Stacy frowned and thought for a moment. Then picked up his knife and fork. "I'll accept that, Howard."

Now with the okay, the rest of the Stacys picked up their forks and begin to eat dinner by first deboning each branzino. As Helen sliced into her fish and began pulling out the very thin bones, she looked over to Peter, who was beside himself with the branzino. "So tell us a little about yourself, Peter."

"Not really much to tell," Peter said, still looking down at the foreign object on his dinner plate.

Captain Stacy's sudden change in tone indicated otherwise. "In my line of work that's a dead giveaway that a man has something to hide."

"Daddy." Gwen shot her dad a piercing look.

"You'll have to forgive my husband, Peter," Helen said, giving her husband the same look. "He sometimes has difficulty determining the difference between a dining room and an interrogation room." Helen noticed Peter's blank stare at the branzino. "Oh, dear, you're struggling aren't you. Simon, help Gwen's friend with his fish."

Ten-year-old Simon reached over and began expertly filleting Peter's branzino.

"I'd just like a little background that's all." Captain Stacy asked. "What's your father do?"

Peter knew this was coming. "I didn't really know my father. I mean, not long, that is. My parents left when I was very young." Peter stopped speaking, but everyone leaned in ever-so-slightly, waiting for more, Captain Stacy included. Silence once again. Gwen couldn't help but sneak a peek at Peter. She, too, wanted to know more about his mysterious past. After all, she had the perfect home, the perfect family, the perfect life. What was it like to not have something as perfect as that? Then Simon returned Peter's fish to him, perfectly filleted.

"It's hard to get the little ones," Simon informed him. "You could still puncture your larynx if one goes down sideways."

"Well," Helen said, clearing her throat, "let's hope that doesn't happen, Simon," Helen continued, trying to take the focus off Peter. "George, why don't you tell us about your day?"

"Yeah, Dad. You find that Spider-Guy yet?" Howard asked.

Captain Stacy shifted a bit in his chair; this was clearly a sensitive subject. "No. But we will. He's an amateur. And I just assigned two of my best detectives to the case."

"Why assign two of your best detectives if he's an amateur?" Peter asked innocently.

Captain Stacy looked over at Peter. He felt a challenge, but wasn't sure. After all, would a high school student dare challenge a police captain in his own home? "I have a masked man who is serially assaulting our citizens at night," Captain Stacy said defiantly, as he cut into his fish. "He's clumsy. He leaves clues. But he's still dangerous."

Peter continued, "I wonder though. Is he really? I mean, I saw that video of the carjacker. I think most people would say he was providing a public service."

Once again, the dinner table grew quiet. All eyes were on Captain Stacy, waiting to see what his next reply would be. The captain continued to cut his fish.

"They'd be wrong. If I'd wanted that carjacker off the streets, he'd be off the streets."

"Why wasn't he then?" Peter said as Captain Stacy looked up and stared dead at Peter. "Sir."

The captain put down his fork and folded his hands. "Let's get something straight, son. I've had enough crackpots telling me how to run my department—"

"Peter's not a crackpot, Dad," Gwen said without missing a beat.

"That carjacker was leading us to the people who run the whole operation," Captain Stacy informed Peter, becoming more defensive with every word. "It's called strategy. Do you understand strategy?"

"Obviously he didn't know you had a plan," Peter replied, trying to ease the growing tension.

"Obviously? Whose side are you on? Do you know something we don't?"

"It was on the Internet," Peter responded nervously. "It looked like he was trying to help."

At this point, Captain Stacy went into full workmode, back in an interrogation room, just like his wife predicted. "Looked like? Looked like? Of course you want to make him out to be a masked hero."

"I doubt he was trying to be a hero," Peter said, growing more and more uncomfortable with the direction of the conversation—but he wanted to be clear on what Spider-Man was really doing. After all, Peter was the wall-crawler in that video. "He was just trying to do something the police couldn't."

Captain Stacy had had enough. "You think we sit around with our thumbs up our—"

"George!" his wife snapped.

"Up your what, Daddy?" a bitter Gwen asked.

The mood at the dinner table had taken a drastic turn, but that didn't seem to stop Peter from getting his point across. "Maybe he stands for what you stand for, sir—stopping the bad guys."

"I stand for potholes!" an enthusiastic Howard added.

Captain Stacy leaned in. "I stand for law and order. I wear a badge. He wears a mask like an outlaw."

"You can't call a man a criminal because he wears a mask," Peter interjected.

"Peter's right, George," Helen stated. "Won't stand up in court."

"You take him to court, counselor. I'm taking him to jail."

"Peter's not your enemy, Daddy," Gwen said, defending Peter.

Captain Stacy frowned. "And who is he anyway? A seventeen-year old boy who I find in *your* room and I don't know *how* he got there? I don't know who he is, except someone that got roughed up. You're full of bruises. You come to dinner dressed in a T-shirt—"

"George, that's enough!" Helen cried.

That *was* enough. Gwen stood and excused herself from dinner. "Let's get some air, Peter," before she left she turned to her father. "You and I need to have a talk, Dad."

Peter stood as well. "Thank you, sir," he said to Captain Stacy. He turned to Mrs. Stacy. "Wonderful branzino." Peter looked over to Howard. "Down with potholes."

Howard smiled and yelled back, "Potholes!"

The dining room slowly cleared out. With his wife

still staring at him with a look only a husband in trouble would recognize, the police captain looked up. "Please pass the peas."

Peter walked out onto the roof of the building. Seconds later, Gwen appeared.

"That was something," she said trying to make light of the situation.

Peter grinned. "I thought he was going to arrest me."

"I wouldn't have let him," Gwen replied. She paused, and then asked, "What did happen to your face?"

Peter looked away, and closed his eyes. "I've been bitten."

Gwen stared at his battered and bruised appearance and replied softly, "So have I . . ."

Realizing she might be talking about something else, he quickly added, "No, well . . . um. It's about the car thief and the vigilante."

He had ruined the moment. "Aw, please not this again," Gwen said walking away.

"I wasn't going to talk about them," he replied, trying to fix the moment. "I was going to talk about me."

Turning to him she replied, "What about you?"

"It's hard to know how to say it."

"Just *say*—"

But before she could finish, Peter kissed her. Their kiss felt like it lasted an eternity, as if they were the only two people in the world. Then a voice called out to Gwen and snapped them back to reality. It was her mother. Gwen turned to answer her and when she turned back around, Peter Parker was gone.

Gwen looked out at the New York City skyline and smiled. Her relationship with Peter Parker had only just begun, and it was already amazing. . . .

THE BIGGEST TEST YET

A LOT CAN happen to someone in just a week. Seventeen-year old Peter Parker was no exception. Just a couple weeks ago, Peter was a normal student at Midtown Science High School: dealing with science and chemistry, being shy around girls, and putting up with the occasional bullying from star athlete Flash Thompson. While visiting Oscorp Tower on a field trip, Peter snuck into a top secret lab, got bit by a strange spider, and suddenly developed superhuman powers; he was able to scale the tallest buildings as easily as if he was walking. He could run really fast and really far. Twenty-seven *miles* far. He could even lift things neither he nor any other normal person should have been able to lift—you know, like, cars and stuff. He even got the girl of his dreams, Gwen Stacy. But with all great things . . . come great problems.

Sidetracked by his newfound powers and ever-changing personality, Peter lost what was most important and dear to him: Uncle Ben. Peter had let a robber get away. Later that night, that same robber ended up killing his uncle, leaving Aunt May a widow. If only Peter could have stopped the robber, Uncle Ben would be alive; he would still be a husband to his high school sweetheart, Aunt May, and a father figure to Peter. But Peter had been selfish. And now he had to deal with the consequences of his choice. That's why he became the Amazing Spider-Man, vowing to stop those who hurt others, and to protect those in need.

Spider-Man used his web-shooters to zip across New York City's famous skyline. Swinging down from one skyscraper, he cut his webbing and did a spectacular aerial flip through the night sky. He shot another web at the adjacent high-rise building and swung around it, clinging sideways to the metal skyscraper, fifty-eight stories above the bustling streets of Lower Manhattan.

As Spider-Man, Peter had become very familiar with his new powers and abilities. But what he didn't know was that Spider-Man was about to be pushed to the limit like never before. . . .

While out patrolling the Lower East Side, Spider-Man saw some bright lights, or what looked like bright lights, coming from the distance. Under his mask, Peter's eyes grew wide with concern. Then they grew even wider with fear. Over the East River, a chaotic scene unfolded on the Williamsburg Bridge. Car after car was being flipped high into the night sky like toys. Some came crashing back down onto the bridge, exploding on impact. Others fell to the icy water below, the fate of the victims inside unknown. Spider-Man could see hundreds of frightened people on the bridge, running for their lives as they avoided the rain of vehicles and debris falling all around them. But then Spider-Man's heightened senses helped him notice something else. This *something* was moving across the bridge at a very high speed. It was too big to be a normal person, but it was not as big as a car. It was a figure that resembled a reptile of some sort. It looked as if it had a tail and a tongue like a lizard . . . and it was causing mass hysteria on the bridge.

Spider-Man had to act fast. And he had to act now! He leaped high into the air and, firing web-shooter after web-shooter, zipped his way toward the Williamsburg Bridge at lightning speed, making it there in no time. Spider-Man looked around for the lizardlike figure that had caused this devastation, but it was long gone. Yet Spider-Man had a gut feeling that he would meet it again. . . .

But Spider-Man didn't have time to think about the future. He had bigger problems right now! Destruction lay everywhere: dozens of mangled and destroyed cars hung off the bridge, ready to crash to the frigid waters below at any moment. Some bobbed in the East River. Others were on fire. Innocent civilians ran in every direction, trying to avoid the chaos all around them. In the distance, Spider-Man could hear helicopters, fire trucks, ambulances, and police cars approaching the Williamsburg Bridge. But there was no way that help was going to arrive in time to save all these people.

Spider-Man knew that he had to act fast and rescue as many people as he could!

Cars that had been tossed close to the bridge's side rails were slowly slipping away. Some were just inches from falling to the cold, black abyss below. Spidey aimed his wrist at a slipping car and fired a web-line at its bumper. Next, he slowly pulled the vehicle back to safety. But he wasn't finished. There were at least a dozen more vehicles in trouble! *Thwip! Thwip! Thwip! Thwip!* One after another, Spider-Man fired his webbing at cars, trucks, and vans, pulling them—and the people inside—out of harm's way. The passengers got out of the cars and ran to safety, some turning back and waving at Spider-Man to thank him for helping them. Underneath his mask, Peter smiled as he waved back. But Spider-Man knew that a Super Hero's job was never done until everyone was saved. Everyone! The wall-crawler looked over the bridge. Several people that had fallen to the icy waters were now on top of a floating car, waving for help. That's when Spidey heard a crunching metal noise. A piece of the bridge was breaking off the guardrail, which was in the direct path of the people below! Suddenly a chunk of metal the size of a small school bus broke away from the bridge and plummeted. Within a millisecond, Spider-Man fired webbing at the falling wreckage. His webbing smacked the piece of metal dead-on, and Spidey began pulling it up. He then swung the slab of metal high above his head and launched it out into the open river, where it splashed far away from any victims.

Spider-Man let out a sigh of relief. But the moment was short-lived. A piercing scream came from below him. A woman was hanging on to the bottom of the bridge! Spider-Man yelled for her to stay calm—but how could she? She was seconds from falling hundreds of feet. Suddenly, her grip on the bridge's metal frame began to loosen. Soon, she let go altogether. In a split second, Spider-Man soared over the side of the bridge and dived to her. He fired his web-shooters at the woman—who was just inches from crashing into the freezing river. *Fwip! Fwip! Fwip!* His webs wrapped around her wrists and he yanked up on the lines, catapulting them up and over the overpass, where they landed safely.

All around Spider-Man, screams rang out. He looked down and saw one of the hanging vehicles that he had stopped from falling with his web-shooters. Inside, a family called for him to help them escape. He leaped over the side of the bridge and landed hard on the car. It began to violently rock back and forth. Spider-Man knew he needed to act fast or the car would fall. He reached in and grabbed one person. Then another. And another. He told them to hold on, and he shot a web back up to the bridge's suspension towers and ascended to safety. Three more innocent civilians were safe—but there were many more still in trouble.

Back on the bridge, Spider-Man could see a small truck smoldering nearby. Thick black smoke was coming from under the hood. Suddenly, the fire quickly spread from the engine toward the dashboard. Spider-Man took a closer look. There was someone inside—it was a child! She was in the backseat banging on the glass for help! Spider-Man fired his web-shooters at the back door of the truck and ripped it clean off its frame. Then he fired another web-line at the screaming victim and yanked her out of the truck and into his arms just as the truck exploded, sending debris everywhere. When the smoke cleared, the little girl realized that Spider-Man had shielded her from danger. She looked up at him and smiled in amazement. She had been saved by Spider-Man!

Crick! Crack! Spider-Man whipped his head around to see what the crackling noise was. He motioned for the girl to run off to safety, and she did. The cracking was coming from the edge of the bridge. The web-line holding one of the vans over the cold, frigid water was on fire! Spider-Man jumped down to it, but his sudden impact jolted the van and—*CRACK!*—the webbing snapped in two! The van plunged, but Spider-Man reacted with his new super powers. He quickly grabbed the rear bumper with one hand and the end of the broken webbing with the other. Spider-Man held the van in place, his face in pure agony as he started to slowly be stretched out past his body's physical limits. Spider-Man heard a cry for help coming from the van. Someone was inside! But he couldn't tell who or how many! They were moving frantically, trying to escape—but there was nowhere for them to go!

Then Spider-Man noticed smoke from the busted engine starting to fill up the inside of van. Spider-Man scrambled to do something—but what could he do? In one hand, he held a piece of webbing that was slowly slipping from his grip; in the other, a van on fire with someone inside. His hands were literally full.

Suddenly, the wind picked up and began to push the van to the left. Then to the right. Spider-Man let out a muffled scream as his body continued to stretch beyond its capacity. His face strained and every vein in his neck pulsed, ready to burst from the extreme pressure of holding on to a two-ton van. He looked to the icy river below and could see people screaming. Peter had to help them! Spider-Man had to help them! But how? What was he to do? If he let go of the car, the person or people inside would fall. But if he didn't help the people in the water, they would freeze. Meanwhile, explosions continued to rock the Williamsburg Bridge, sending shockwaves down through the web to Spider-Man. The web was ready to break at any moment!

As Spider-Man held on to the car for dear life, random thoughts began to flash before him: playing hide-and-seek with his father back in his dad's old office; Aunt May sitting at the kitchen table alone, waiting for Peter to come home; Uncle Ben telling him that with great power comes great responsibility; the spider bite he received at Oscorp; discovering his newfound abilities; falling in love with Gwen Stacy. Finally, his thoughts turned to whatever had caused this traumatic scene. He thought about how Spider-Man would search high above the New York skyline and deep below the sewers of Manhattan to find this threat. This monster. Peter was more determined than ever to save the rest of the people on the bridge and those in the water. Then he would find this menace and stop it, because it was his responsibility as a New Yorker, a Super Hero . . . and as the Amazing Spider-Man!

colleagues had indeed high hopes that this...
a problem had been rising for years. He...

STORY 9:

SPIDER-MAN VERSUS THE LIZARD

"**SUBJECT: DR. CURTIS CONNORS**, current temperature: 89.7 degrees Fahrenheit, steady for forty-eight hours," said Dr. Connors in a calm voice. If anyone had told him two weeks ago that he would be conducting the greatest experiment of his life . . . actually, he probably would have believed them. Dr. Connors was one of the nation's most brilliant geneticists and the head of Oscorp's science division, after all.

However, if someone told him he'd be conducting those experiments in a makeshift lab hidden in the sewers of New York, he would have said they were insane! It had been an eventful couple of weeks. First, Peter Parker, the son of one of Dr. Connors's former colleagues, had unknowingly helped Dr. Connors solve a problem he'd been facing for years. He had been trying to transfer the regenerative powers of common lizards into human beings, something which would help countless people recover from injuries.

He personally knew exactly how much this could help people. Dr. Connors had lost his right arm a long time ago, and he wanted to benefit from this kind of scientific breakthrough. He *knew* it would work—after all, it had already worked once. Kind of. The first time Dr. Connors experimented on himself, he watched in silent amazement as his arm grew back! But there were more changes in store for Dr. Connors—the reptilian DNA raged through his body, changing him into a dangerously unstable creature. This creature was no longer Dr. Connors, it was only the Lizard!

As the Lizard, he was powerful. After he had fully transformed, he felt better than he had in his entire life. After feeling incomplete for so long, he felt better than 100 percent. He wanted to share that feeling with the world. He was unstoppable and he knew it, and he was angry with the world after being held back for so long. The rage built, resulting in the Lizard attacking parts of the city. It was only through the efforts of

Spider-Man, and the city's police force, that innocent lives were saved from the Lizard's rampage.

But the change didn't last. The Lizard turned back into Dr. Connors, who lost his superhuman abilities—and his regrown arm. Dr. Connors was horrified by what he had done. But he saw one shining light of hope: his formula worked! He had regrown his missing arm! He knew that he was smart enough to figure out how to permanently grow back the arm without becoming the Lizard again. He had taken equipment from his job at Oscorp and disappeared into the night, determined to finish what he had begun. He wasn't willing to listen to warnings about the dangers—deep down, he didn't even care about the dangers. He had to complete this experiment, no matter the cost.

And that is how Dr. Connors, dedicated father and world-famous scientist, ended up recording his lab notes in a hidden corner of the sewers. The only witness to his continued experiments was a lab rat named Fred. Fred was the only other being that had been exposed to Dr. Connors's formula. Dr. Connors continued dictating the details of his experiments into a small video camera: "Blood panels reveal lymphocyte and monocyte readings consistent with subject's past." His exposure to the reptilian DNA made some changes that stuck with him, even after he returned to human form.

"Blood-clotting rate vastly improved, marked enhancement in muscle response, strength, and elasticity. Eyesight similarly improved; subject no longer requires corrective lenses. Current daily dosage, administered three times daily, is one hundred milligrams." Dr. Connors took a deep breath and got ready for the next step. This will work, he told himself. This will work, and nothing will ever be the same again!

He looked over at the plastic cage that Fred the rat was sitting in. Fred looked back at him. The rat seemed stronger and more alert than ever. "Regenerative effects in animal trial were successful and sustained," said Dr. Connors as he watched the rat scamper around in its cage. "There is no expectation of relapse. Animal subject is biologically whole." Dr. Connors knew it was time to move forward with the next stage of the experiment: it was time to test the revised formula on himself! He shackled his legs to the pipes of the sewer, just in case the Lizard emerged again, and he picked up the hypodermic needle with the next stage of the formula in it. "In attempt to redress regenerative relapse, dosage has been increased to two hundred milligrams." He took another deep breath. "Human trials begin," he said as he plunged the needle into his thigh.

Far away from Dr. Connors's experiment, the people of New York were living in fear of a creature few had even seen. No one quite knew what to make of the rumors that a half-man, half-lizard monster was running loose in the Big Apple, but people were taking to the streets trying to stop him. Since the Lizard disappeared, many would-be reptile hunters were patrolling the banks of the East River, trying to track down the beast.

The same evening Dr. Connors was testing the formula on himself, the main news stories were all Lizard, all the time. "Self-appointed vigilantes have taken to the streets in Queens, Brooklyn, and as far away as Rockville Centre in search of the rumored killing beast," said the lead anchor on the evening news.

Peter Parker watched the news from his room in

Queens. He knew that Dr. Connors was the Lizard. Peter also knew that with his new abilities, the Amazing Spider-Man was the only person who would be able to stop the Lizard. He was still worried. I may be superstrong and quick, Peter thought, but that thing was tossing cars off of the bridge like they were made of paper!

As he loaded cartridges into his wrist-mounted web-shooters, he started coming up with a plan. I have abilities like a spider—maybe I should try thinking like a spider, Peter said to himself. He put on his Spider-Man costume, finished loading webbing into his web-shooters, and quietly snuck out of the house. Aunt May would never be okay with me putting myself in danger, thought Peter. But there's no other way. If I don't find Dr. Connors before the Lizard attacks again, people will get hurt—people could die.

Spider-Man swung through the night and headed toward the last place he had seen the Lizard. He knew Dr. Connors was hiding somewhere in the sewer system, but finding him was going to be tricky. Spidey easily picked up a manhole cover and jumped into the sewers. Spider-Man was still getting used to his new powers, and for every awesome thing, such as being able to lift manhole covers with his little finger, there was something decidedly less awesome. For example: crawling around in the city's forgotten underground tunnels.

It was time to put his latest bright idea to the test. Finding a hublike area of the sewers where numerous tunnels met, Spider-Man started shooting webbing as far as it would go down the various tunnels. Over and over and over again, faster than a normal person's eye would be able to follow, Spidey made what had to be the biggest spiderweb the world had ever seen. He thought that if he could make a giant early-detection system for anything wandering through the tunnels, he'd be able to tell when anyone was moving, just like a real spider would do with insects it was trying to catch!

But, as they say, the waiting is the hardest part. Spider-Man crouched acrobatically at the heart of his giant web, took a deep breath, and waited. And waited. And waited some more. He thought about Aunt May, and how much he missed Uncle Ben. He thought about the homework he'd have to catch up on if he lived through hunting down the Lizard. He thought about Gwen and how much he was looking forward to talking to her again. He thought about how he was getting kind of hungry, and how he'd been down in the sewers for a while now, and how he'd really, really like to head to a diner and get some pancakes. . . .

Spider-Man couldn't wait any longer. Even still, he had to keep the element of surprise on his side, so as he climbed along the walls and ceilings of the tunnel, he kept to the shadows. He followed the trail through the tunnels. He knew that he was getting close, but it was a dark and claustrophobic place.

As he scampered upside-down along the roof of a tunnel, Spider-Man saw a large shadow coming from around a corner, up ahead. Gotcha, he thought. Time to take this guy down. Just as he started to get close, his spider-sense started going off like crazy! Where is he? Peter wondered. But before he could whirl around and check behind him, a giant claw came out of the darkness and lashed at Spider-Man's chest. Spidey was able to dodge the brunt of the hit, but he was knocked back—HARD. Spider-Man regained his footing and looked down. A giant claw tore across his new red and blue costume, ruining the spider emblem on his chest. His spider-sense went off again and he immediately rolled backward, avoiding another blow. Spider-Man quickly shot to his feet, looking to get back on the ceiling where he'd be out of the Lizard's reach. He hadn't even fully seen the creature yet, and he already knew this was going to be the toughest fight of his life!

Before Spidey could get to the top of the tunnel, he was once again knocked back to the ground by this strange force. Spider-Man landed in a puddle on the sewer's floor and groaned in pain. What had hit him this time? he thought. His spider-sense was still going off like crazy, but it was too dark in this part of the tunnel to even see where the attacks were coming from. A dark figure seemed to be lurking all around the web-crawler. A low hiss came from behind Spider-Man. Spidey looked left. Then right. This monster was everywhere! For every blow Spider-Man was able to block, another one found its mark, and he quickly found himself reeling. Then, something swung right at Spider-Man's head and cracked him upside the skull.

He fell to his knees. That's when he saw the beast for the first time.

Spider-Man gasped. He knew that Dr. Connors's transformation would be startling, but nothing could have prepared him for what he saw. Dr. Connors's formula had succeeded in changing him back into the Lizard: a gigantic monster who loomed over Spider-Man. Even if Spider-Man was able to land a blow, he wasn't sure if the Lizard would even feel it!

Spider-Man tried to swing away to a place where he could catch his breath and figure out how to make a dent in the Lizard's powerful form, but the Lizard grabbed him from behind and hurled him into a brick wall. Spider-Man staggered to his knees again. Maybe this wasn't such a good idea after all, he thought, as the Lizard's hand closed around his throat. Just then he looked into the Lizard's eyes and realized something. They looked just like Dr. Connors's eyes! Maybe the man was still somewhere in the monster after all. If Peter could just find a way to reason with the Lizard, maybe—just maybe—the Lizard would revert back to its human form and become Dr. Connors again.

"Wait, Doc, it's—" Spider-Man began, but before he could finish, he was knocked back by the Lizard's powerful tail. The last thing Peter remembered thinking before he blacked out was: so much for that idea.

When Spider-Man came to, the Lizard was gone. Spidey picked up the remains of his costume that had been clawed at by the Lizard, and headed back to the streets. He didn't know why the Lizard didn't finish him off, but either way, he knew he had to find this monster and stop him. But before he did anything else, he was going to have to find a first-aid kit.

I don't know if I can take him in a fight, thought Spider-Man, but Dr. Connors is clearly still in there. I know I can save him. But I can't do it alone . . .

And with that, Spider-Man swung into the night, as determined as ever.

BATTLE AT MIDTOWN SCIENCE HIGH

DR. CONNORS HAD never felt better. He had never felt more focused. He didn't care about the state of the world, or whether his lab supplies were going to come in on time, or what his wife and son were doing. As he stared at his hands—his two hands, his two green, scaly, perfect and powerful hands—the only thing he cared about was the one person who could ruin his newfound perfection.

Spider-Man.

Spider-Man wanted to stop *the Lizard*. He was the only one who could.

He had to find Spider-Man. He had to crush Spider-Man and make sure that no one could stop Dr. Connors, no one could stop the Lizard, from being whole. And he knew just how to do it. Crouched far beneath the streets of New York, the Lizard stood completely still. He didn't know who Spider-Man was. But he knew how to find the Super Hero. Spider-Man had appeared when the Lizard had gone on a rampage on the Williamsburg Bridge, so the Lizard knew that if he started causing trouble, Spider-Man would appear again. He just needed to find the best place . . . and a high school filled with innocent children seemed like a good place to start!

Spider-Man had found the Lizard in the sewers, and the Lizard had nearly killed him. He couldn't even remember why he hadn't finished the web-slinger off, but he knew that was a mistake he wouldn't make again.

Dr. Connors's transformation into the Lizard had done more than allow him to regrow his missing arm and turn into an eight foot-tall mass of scales and muscle; it had done more than give him a powerful tail to use for balance and attack. It had also given him an intense hunter's instinct. With the single-minded determination of a predator at the top of the food chain, the Lizard quickly moved through the tunnels beneath the city.

Nothing was going to stand in his way.

At Midtown Science High, two girls were gossiping in the ladies room before their third-period class began.

"I know, right?" one said to the other. "Why does she think she can make out with him and still be friends with me? That's it, I'm never talking to her again!"

Just then, the bathroom started to shake. The girls looked around, but it was impossible to tell where the rumbling was coming from.

"What's going on?!?" the second girl screamed to her friend.

With a massive thud, the ground shook, and one of the stalls in the bathroom disappeared into a hole in the floor! Everything was quiet for a second, and the two stared slack-jawed at the small crater in the floor of their school. And then they saw something they had never seen before—and never wanted to see again. The Lizard jumped through the opening in the floor and landed before the two girls, smashing everything around him!

The girls screamed at the top of their lungs, as they ran out of the bathroom and into the hall. The Lizard didn't care about them—he knew he was close to finding Spider-Man and taking care of the only problem he had left.

Minutes earlier, Peter Parker and Gwen Stacy had walked into Midtown Science High School. Like the beast hunting him down, Peter found himself focused. He knew the Lizard was out there somewhere. He was worried about what would happen the next time they met, and he was still sad about the loss of his Uncle Ben. It had been a crazy few weeks, after all. But more than anything, he was just happy to be walking into Midtown Science High hand-in-hand with Gwen Stacy. It made him feel like—whatever happened next—everything was going to be okay.

And he was going to get the chance to find out if he was right sooner than he could have imagined. An explosion down the hall from where Gwen and Peter were standing shook them both out of their daze. All they could see was a cloud of dust, and all they could hear were the screams of their fellow students, but Peter knew instantly what had happened. The Lizard was here. But Peter was ready this time. He had his Spider-Man costume in his backpack, and he was already wearing his web-shooters underneath his long-sleeved shirt.

Peter headed into the stream of fleeing students. "Peter!" Gwen shouted. "Where are you going? We need to get out of here!" But Peter knew he needed to change into his Spider-Man costume to protect his secret identity, but he knew he also had to try and keep his fellow students safe while they were evacuating the building. Even Flash Thompson deserved better than getting pummeled by an eight-foot-tall lizard monster.

Gwen was busy trying to clear the hall and was not paying attention to him, so Peter quickly cut through the crowd. He saw the Lizard at the end of the hall. There were still some kids running down the hall, dangerously close to the Lizard. Peter sprinted toward the creature, sliding on his knees as he got close. Without anyone seeing him, Peter shot an ankle-high line of webbing across the floor as he passed by the Lizard. The creature was tripped up by the web-line, but Peter's backpack went skidding across the floor. Peter was right next to the lab used for the advanced chemistry class, which was empty. If he could just grab his backpack, he could duck in there and change without any of the fleeing students seeing.

"Everyone hide! Get out of here!" yelled Peter. He was still on the ground, but he had to get that backpack! Peter reached out his arm to shoot a web-line at it, but the Lizard was already back on his feet, and a scaly foot came down on Peter's arm before he could get the backpack. The Lizard loomed over Peter in the hall and let out a terrifying roar.

Some boys and girls that Peter recognized from the basketball teams were herding younger students toward the exits, but it was clear the kids were going to need more time. Peter had to get everyone to safety and change into his Spider-Man costume—and he needed to do it fast, without anyone seeing him!

Behind the Lizard, Peter could see Gwen running toward them. She had made it through the crowd of students, which was much easier now, as most kids wanted to be as far from the monster as possible!

"Hey!" Gwen yelled at the top of her lungs at the

Lizard. "Get away from him!" The Lizard lifted his leg off Peter's arm and turned toward Gwen. Her distraction worked! She turned and headed down the hall, following the other students running out of the school.

Peter's spider-sense was tingling like crazy as he shot to his feet and grabbed his backpack out of the nearby rubble. He turned just in time to see the Lizard's giant arm heading toward him. The next thing Peter knew, he was lying in a pile of dust and janitor's equipment, staring at the Lizard through a person-size hole in the wall.

Yep, Peter thought, as he pulled on his Spider-Man costume as quickly as he could, the Lizard's still pretty darn strong.

Down the hall near the exit, Gwen turned around just in time to see the Lizard stalk toward the wall. Just then, a web-line shot out of the hole in the wall and Spider-Man, fully dressed and ready for action, drop-kicked the Lizard in the chest and somersaulted away.

Spidey dusted some rubble off of his sleeve as he landed. "Okay," he said aloud to himself, "if I survive this, I know I can get dressed in eight seconds . . . as long as there's a lizard-beast-man trying to eat me."

The Lizard roared in frustrated rage at Spider-Man's continued knack for survival. Spider-Man had learned a thing or two from his fight with the Lizard in the sewers. Every time the Lizard approached, Spider-Man made sure to stay clear of his powerful arms and especially his tail. Spider-Man tried to shoot a line of webbing over the Lizard's eyes, but the Lizard moved faster than Spidey thought was possible, dodging the webbing and using his tail to slam Spider-Man against the lockers along one side of the hallway.

Spider-Man struggled to get a hand around the Lizard's tail. He pushed as hard as he could and heard a THWACK! The Lizard's grip loosened, and Spider-Man was able to pry himself away from the monster. He saw the Lizard holding the back of his head, a broken giant football trophy on the ground, and Gwen running away from the fight. She had snuck up behind the Lizard and clocked him.

His head's not as tough as the rest of him, Spidey thought. That's good to know. But I've gotta get Gwen out of here!

Spider-Man swung and landed next to Gwen, but the Lizard was hot on their heels. Peter had to keep his identity a secret, but he knew he needed to keep Gwen safe, too!

"Hey," he said, grabbing Gwen. "Everyone else has escaped. I can take care of this now. You need to get out of here." Then he pushed her down the hall and ran back toward the Lizard.

"Thank you, Spider-Man!" Gwen yelled over her shoulder as she ran downstairs toward the main doors. As much as she wanted to help, she knew that only Spider-Man had a chance of stopping the Lizard's rampage.

Back upstairs, Spider-Man went flying through the doors of the library, the Lizard snarling right behind him. Spidey rolled under the Lizard's charge and used the giant's momentum against him, tossing him straight into a stack of books. The other stacks nearby collapsed on the Lizard too, but that didn't hold him for long! The scaly monster burst from the books and headed at high speed straight for Spider-Man!

Spidey knew that this fight wasn't going to end well.

Even in daylight and with room to dodge, the Lizard was far too powerful to be knocked unconscious. And even if Spidey could knock him out, what then? It's not like he could ask Captain Stacy to bring the economy-size handcuffs down. The police may be forced to kill the Lizard, and the Lizard certainly wouldn't mind killing the police. The only way to keep everyone safe was to try and reach Dr. Connors. The real Dr. Connors, not the creature he had become.

Spider-Man backed out of the library, and the Lizard stomped toward him. Spider-Man kept his arms in front of him, ready to move but trying to appeal to the human being that he hoped was still in there. "Dr. Connors!" he yelled. "Are you still in there? Can you hear me?"

The Lizard angrily shook his head and lashed his tail at Spider-Man, but Spidey was able to back-flip out of the way. Just then, the Lizard ran away. Spider-Man cautiously headed into the hallway. He was ready for the Lizard to attack again, but oddly, there was no sign of him. By the time Spidey caught up with the creature, it had turned back into Dr. Connors!

The sirens were getting closer and closer, and Peter knew he and Dr. Connors had to act fast if they were going to find a way to keep the Lizard from re-emerging. It was time for Dr. Connors to return to his subterranean lab—but it was anyone's guess if they could unlock the formula that created the Lizard in time!

"Let's go," said Spider-Man. Whatever was going to happen, he knew that he'd help his friend, no matter what. They found Dr. Connors a pair of sweatpants from one of the lockers that had broken during the fight, and they quickly retreated out of the school.

Dr. Connors could only stare in fearful awe at the destruction he had unleashed. A part of him wanted to have that power back, the feeling that he could do *anything* that coursed through him when he was the Lizard. But he knew that Spider-Man was right. For the sake of those closest to him, Dr. Connors had to find a way to stop the Lizard once and for all.

Peter knew that, just as he had risked his life fighting the Lizard to keep people safe, he would do whatever it took to help Dr. Connors. He wasn't sure what they would do next. But if it meant protecting Dr. Connors from the people who would hurt him, well, that's what would be done. He knew they'd have to act fast, whatever the plan was going to be.

I hope Dr. Connors can pull this off, thought Spider-Man. But whatever happens next, I know this is the right thing to do. Not just for him and his family, but for Gwen and her family, and Aunt May, and the whole city.

Man, I hope this works. . . .